THE
RESURRECTION
OF JIMBER-JAW

(Fantasy and Horror Classics)

By

EDGAR RICE BURROUGHS

First published in 1937

Read & Co.

Copyright © 2022 Fantasy and Horror Classics

This edition is published by Fantasy and Horror Classics,
an imprint of Read & Co.

This book is copyright and may not be reproduced or copied in any
way without the express permission of the publisher in writing.

British Library Cataloguing-in-Publication Data
A catalogue record for this book is available
from the British Library.

Read & Co. is part of Read Books Ltd.
For more information visit
www.readandcobooks.co.uk

CONTENTS

Edgar Rice Burroughs. 5

I. 11

II. 13

III 21

IV 29

V 33

EDGAR RICE BURROUGHS

Edgar Rice Burroughs was born in Chicago in 1875. His father, a Civil War veteran, sent him to Michigan Military Academy in his youth, but in 1895 Burroughs failed the entrance exam for the US army, and was then discharged from the military altogether in 1897 having been diagnosed with a heart problem. Following this, Burroughs worked in a range of unrelated short-term jobs, such as railroad policeman, business partner, and miner. In 1911, having worked for seven years on menial wages, and having taken an interest in the pulp magazines of the day, Burroughs began to write fiction.

Only a year later, Burroughs' story 'Under the Moons of Mars' was serialized in *All-Story Magazine*, earning him $400 (approximately twenty times that by modern-day economic standards). This money enabled Burroughs to start writing full-time and in the same year (1912), he published his successful and most well-known work—*Tarzan of the Apes*. Tarzan was a national sensation, and Burroughs showed an entrepreneurial streak when he exploited it in a range of different ways, from comics to movies to merchandise. By 1923, Burroughs had founded his own company – Edgar Rice Burroughs, Inc. – and printed his own books throughout the rest of his life.

During World War II, as a resident of Hawaii at the time of the Pearl Harbour attack, Burroughs became one of the oldest war correspondents in the US. After the war, Burroughs moved back to California, where he eventually died of a heart attack, leaving behind more than sixty novels. The figure of Tarzan remains immensely popular, and today the original 1912 novel has almost innumerable sequels across all forms of media.

*Bookplate designed for Edgar Rice Burroughs
by his nephew, Studley Oldham Burroughs, in 1922.*

February 4th 1922 sj

Mr. Ruthven Deane,
1222 N. State St.,
Chicago, Ill.

My dear Mr. Deane:

In accordance with your request of January 30th, I am en-
closing herewith copy of my bookplate. The designer is my
nephew, Mr. Studley Oldham Burroughs.

The central figure in the bookplate represents Tarzan. He
is holding the planet Mars, above which are the two Martian
satellites. These because of my Martian series of stories.
Grasping his legs is one of the great apes, among which
Tarzan was reared. In the background are characters from
several of my other stories.

The crossed quill and sabre refer respectively to my writing
and to my service in the United States Cavalry. These are
again referred to in the shield in the spurred boot and the
open volume. The steer's skull in the upper right hand quarter
of the shield represents the time I spent in Idaho riding for
a cow outfit. In the lower left hand quarter the automobile
wheel refers to my love of motoring. Below the shield are my
nephew's initials.

My nephew designed this bookplate at my request, but entirely
without any suggestions from me. Altogether it seems to me
an unusually interesting piece of work.

Yours very truly,

Born, 1875,

*1922 letter between Edgar Rice Burroughs
and Ruthven Deane that describes the details
of the bookplate's design and their relevance.*

7

THE
RESURRECTION
OF JIMBER-JAW

I

Credit this story to Wild Pat Morgan, that laughing, reckless black-haired grandson of Ireland's peat bogs.

To Pat Morgan, one-time flying lieutenant of the AEF, ex-inventor, amateur boxer, and drinking companion *par excellence*.

I met Pat Morgan at the country club bar, one of those casual things. After the third highball we were calling each other by our first names. By the sixth we had dragged the family skeletons out of the closet and were shaking the dust off them. A little later we were weeping on one another's shoulders, and that's how it began.

We got pretty well acquainted that evening, and afterwards our friendship grew. We saw a lot of each other when he brought his ship to the airport where I kept mine. His wife was dead, and he was a rather lonely figure evenings; so I used to have him up to the house for dinner often.

He had been rather young when the war broke out, but had managed to get to France and the front just before the end. I think he shot down three enemy planes, although he was just a kid. I had that from another flyer; Pat never talked about it. But he was full of flying anecdotes about other war-time pilots and about his own stunting experiences in the movies. He had followed this latter profession for several years.

All of which has nothing to do with the real story other than to explain how I became well enough acquainted with Pat Morgan to be on hand when he told the strange tale of his flight to Russia, of the scientist who mastered time, of the man from 50,000 BC called Jimber-Jaw.

We were lunching together at The Vendome that day. I had

been waiting for Pat at the bar, discussing with some others the disappearance of Stone, the wrestler. Everyone is familiar, of course, with Stone's meteoric rise to fame as an athlete and a high-salaried star in the movies, and his vanishing had become a minor ten-days' wonder. We were trying to decide if Stone had been kidnapped, whether the ransom letters received were the work of cranks, when Pat Morgan came in with the extra edition of the *Herald and Express* that the newsboys were hawking in the streets.

I followed Pat to our table and he spread the paper out. A glaring headline gave the meat of the story.

"So they've found him!" I exclaimed.

Pat Morgan nodded. "The police had me in on it. I've just come from Headquarters." He shrugged, frowned, and then began to talk slowly.

II

I've always been inclined to putter around with inventions (Pat Morgan said), and after my wife died I tried to forget my loneliness by centring my interest on my laboratory work. It was a poor substitute for the companionship I had lost, but at that I guess it proved my salvation.

I was working on a new fuel which was much cheaper and less bulky than gasoline; but I found that it required radical changes in engine design, and I lacked the capital to put my blue-prints into metal.

About this time my grandfather died and left me a considerable fortune. Quite a slice of it went into experimental engines before I finally perfected one. It was a honey.

I built a ship and installed my engine in it; then I tried to sell the patents on both engine and fuel to the Government—but something happened. When I reached a certain point in these official negotiations I ran into an invisible stone wall—I was stopped dead. I couldn't even get a permit to manufacture my engine.

I never did find out who or what stopped me, but I remembered the case of the Doble steam car. Perhaps you will recall that, also.

Then I got sore and commenced to play around with the Russians. The war-winds were already beginning to blow again in Europe, and the comrades of the Soviet were decidedly interested in new aircraft developments. They had money to burn, and their representatives had a way with them that soothed the injured ego of a despondent inventor. They finally made me a splendid offer to take my plans and formula to Moscow and manufacture engines and fuel for them. In

13

addition, as a publicity and propaganda stunt, they offered a whacking bonus if I would put my new developments to test by *flying* there.

I jumped at this chance to make monkeys out of those bureaucratic boneheads in Washington. I'd show those guys what they were missing.

During the course of these negotiations I met Dr Stade who was also flirting with the brethren of the USSR. Professor Marvin Stade, to give him his full name and title, and he was quite a guy. A big fellow, built like an ox, with a choleric temper and the most biting pair of blue eyes I've ever gazed upon. You must have read in the papers about Stade's experiments with frozen dogs and monkeys. He used to freeze them up solid for days and weeks, and then thaw them out and bring them alive again. He had also been conducting some unique studies in surgical hypnosis, and otherwise stepping on the toes of the constituted medical Poo-Bahs.

The SPCA and the Department of Health had thrown a monkey- wrench into Stade's programme—stopped him cold—and there was fire in his eye. We were a couple of soreheads, perhaps, but I think we had a right to be. Lord knows we were both sincere in what we were trying to accomplish—he to fight disease, I to add something to the progress of aviation.

The Reds welcomed Dr Stade with open arms. They agreed not only to let him carry his experiments as far as he liked but to finance him as well. They even promised to let him use human beings as subjects and to furnish said humans in job lots. I suppose they had a large supply of counter-revolutionists on hand.

When Stade found that I planned to fly my ship to Moscow, he asked if he might go along. He was a showman as well as a scientist, and the publicity appealed to him. I told him the risk was too great, that I didn't want to take the responsibility of any life other than my own, but he pooh-poohed every objection in that bull-bellow voice of his. Finally I shrugged and said okay.

I won't bore you with the details of the flight. You couldn't have read about it in the papers, of course, for the word went out through official channels that we were to get a cold shoulder. The press put a blanket of silence on us, and that was that. There were passport difficulties, refusals to certify the plane, all that sort of thing. But we managed to muddle through.

The engine functioned perfectly. So did the fuel. So did everything, including my navigation, until we were flying over the most God-forsaken terrain anyone ever saw—some place in Northern Siberia according to our maps. That's where my new-fangled carburettor chose to go haywire.

We had about ten thousand feet elevation at the time, but that wasn't much help. There was no place to land. As far as I could see there was nothing but forests and rivers—hundreds of rivers.

I went into a straight glide with a tail-wind, figuring I could cover a lot more territory that way than I could by spiralling; and every second I was keeping my eyes peeled for a spot, however small, where I might set her down without damage. We'd never get out of that endless forest, I knew, unless we flew out.

I've always liked trees—a nature-lover at heart—but as I looked down on that vast host of silent sentinels of the wilderness, I felt the chill of fear and something that was akin to hate. There was a loneliness and an emptiness inside me. There they stood—in regiments, in divisions, in armies, waiting to seize us and hold us forever; to hold our broken bodies, for when we struck them, they would crush us, tear us to pieces.

Then I saw a little patch of yellow far ahead. It was no larger than the palm of my hand, it seemed, but it was an open space—a tiny sanctuary in the very heart of the enemy's vast encampment. As we approached, it grew larger until at last it resolved itself into a few acres of reddish yellow soil devoid of trees. It was the most beautiful landscape I have ever seen.

As the ship rolled to a stop on fairly level ground, I turned and looked at Dr Stade. He was lighting a cigarette. He paused, with the match still burning, and grinned at me. I knew then that he was regular. It's funny but neither one of us had spoken since the motor quit. That was as it should have been; for there was nothing to say—at least nothing that would have meant anything.

We got down and looked around. Beside us, a little river ran north to empty finally into the Arctic Ocean. Our tiny patch of salvation lay in a bend on the west side of the river. On the east side was a steep cliff that rose at least three hundred feet above the river. The lowest stratum looked like dirty glass. Above that were strata of conglomerate and sedimentary rock; and, topping all, the grim forest scowled down upon us menacingly.

"Funny looking rock," I commented, pointing towards the lowest ledge.

"Ice," said Stade. "My friend, you are looking at the remnants of the late lamented glacial period that raised havoc with the passing of the Pleistocene. What are we going to use for food?"

"We got guns," I reminded him.

"Yes. It was very thoughtful of you to get permission to bring firearms and ammunition, but what are we going to shoot?"

I shrugged. "There must be something. What are all these trees for? They must have been put here for birds to sit on. In the meantime we've sandwiches and a couple of thermoses of hot coffee. I hope it's hot."

"So do I."

It wasn't . . .

I took a shotgun and hunted up river. I got a hare—mostly fur and bones—and a brace of birds that resembled partridges. By the time I got back to camp the weather had become threatening. There was a storm north of us. We could see the lightning, and faint thunder began to growl.

We had already wheeled the plane to the west and highest part of our clearing and staked it down as close under the shelter of the forest as we could. Nothing else to do.

By the time we had cooked and eaten our supper it commenced to rain. The long, northern twilight was obliterated by angry clouds that rolled low out of the north. Thunder bombarded us. Lightning laid down a barrage of pale brilliance all about. We crawled into the cabin of the plane and spread our mattresses and blankets on the floor behind the seats.

It rained. And when I say it rained, I mean it *rained*. It could have given ancient Armenia seven-and-a-half honour tricks and set it at least three; for what it took forty days and forty nights to do in ancient Armenia, it did in one night on that nameless river somewhere in Siberia, USSR. I'll never forget that downpour.

I don't know how long I slept, but when I awoke it was raining not cats and dogs only, but the entire animal kingdom. I crawled out and looked through a window. The next flash of lightning showed the river swirling within a few feet of the outer wing.

I shook Dr Stade awake and called his attention to the danger of our situation.

"The devil!" he said. "Wait till she floats." He turned over and went to sleep again. Of course it wasn't his ship, and perhaps he was a strong swimmer; I wasn't.

I lay awake most of what was left of the night. The rising flood was a foot deep around the landing gear at the worst; then she commenced to go down.

The next morning the river was running in a new channel a few yards from the ship, and the cliff had receded at least fifty feet towards the east. The face of it had fallen into the river and been washed away. The lowest stratum was pure and gleaming ice.

"That's interesting," he said. "By any chance is there any partridge or hare left?"

There was and we ate it. Then we got out and sloshed around in the mud. I started to work on the carburettor. Stade studied the havoc wrought by the storm.

He was down by the edge of the river at the new cliff when he called to me excitedly. I had never before seen the burly professor exhibit any enthusiasm except when he was damning the SPCA and the health authorities. I went on the run.

I could see nothing to get excited about. "What's eating you?" I asked.

"Come here, you dumb Irishman, and see a man fifty thousand years old, or thereabouts." Stade was mainly Scottish and German, which may have accounted for his crazy sense of humour.

I was worried. I thought maybe it might be the heat, but there wasn't any heat. No more could it have been the altitude; so I figured it must be hereditary, and crawled down and walked over to him.

"Look!" he said. He pointed across the river at the cliff.

I looked—and there it was. Frozen into the solid ice, was the body of a man. He was clothed in furs and had a mighty beard. He lay on his side with his head resting on one arm, as though he were soundly sleeping.

Stade was awe struck. He just stood there, goggle-eyed, staring at the corpse. Finally he drew in his breath in a long sigh.

"Do you realise, Pat, that we are looking at a man who may have lived fifty thousand years ago, a survivor of the old Stone Age?"

"What a break for you, Doc," I said.

"Break for me? What do you mean?"

"You can thaw him out and bring him to life."

He looked at me in a sort of a blank way, as though he didn't comprehend what I was saying. His lips moved, mumbling, then he shook his head.

"I'm afraid he's been frozen too long," he said.

"Fifty thousand years is quite a while, but wouldn't it be worth trying? Keep you busy while I'm fixing things to get us out of here."

Again he fixed his blank stare upon me. His eyes were as cold and expressionless as that distant cliff of ice. "All right, Paddy me boy," he said suddenly. "But you'll have to help me."

III

My suggestion was a joke, of course, but Stade was in deadly earnest once he got started. I wasn't much help, I'm afraid, after the first couple of days, for I came down with a queer combination of chills and fever that had me light-headed most of the time. But I worked when I could.

It took us two weeks to build a rude hut of saplings and chink it with clay. It had a fireplace and a bench for the queer paraphernalia that Stade had brought along—more gadgets than you could shake a stick at. Then it took us another two weeks to chip our cave man out of the ice. We had to be careful; there was danger of breaking him.

I'm the one who gave our corpse his name. There in the ice, with his skin-clad body and his hairy face, he looked like a big lantern- jawed grizzly I'd seen one time up the Yellowstone. Jimber-Jaw had been the grizzly's name, and that's what I called our discovery. That fever had me so dizzy, I tell you, that I felt like a man on a spree most of the time.

Anyway, we worked all around our frozen subject, leaving him encased in a small block of the glacier. Then we lowered him to the ground, floated him across the river, and dragged him up to the laboratory on a crude sled we had built for that purpose.

All the time we were working on him we did a lot of thinking. I kept on treating the whole thing as a sort of joke, but Stade grew more grimly serious with every day. He worked with a furious driving energy that swept me along. Nights, by the fire, he would talk on and on about the memories that were locked in that frozen brain. What sights had those ice-cased eyes beheld in the days when the world was young? What loves, what hates had stirred that mighty breast?

Here was a creature that had lived in the days of the mammoth and the sabre-tooth and the great flying monsters. He had survived against the odds, with only a stone spear and a stone knife against a predatory world, until the cold of the great glacier had captured and overpowered him.

Stade said he had been hunting and that he had been caught in a blizzard. Numb with cold, he had at last dropped down on the chill ice, succumbing to that inevitable urge to sleep that overtakes all freezing men. For fifty thousand years he had slept on, undisturbed. (Lord, how I sometimes envied him!)

I was pretty well played out by the time the final test arrived. My temperature was well past 102 degrees, and I walked around in a semi-delirium most of the morning. But Stade insisted that he needed me, that I had to stay on my feet. He crammed me full of quinine and whisky and I went on a singing jag. I remembered the words to some of the old songs that I thought I'd forgotten.

That's why there are parts of that day that I remember distinctly and other parts that are only a hazy blank.

Stade built a roaring blaze in the fireplace and our laboratory-hut was oven warm. The propeller of the plane, idling, kept the air of the room in circulation, blowing wind through an opening in the wall that had been built for that purpose. I helped to prop our subject in front of the fire, then slumped back, all groggy, and left the rest to Stade. It was his picnic.

He kept turning Jimber-Jaw over—first one side then the other towards the fire—until the ice was all melted. Then the body commenced to warm.

I stopped my singing long enough to get sensible. I shook the fog out of my brain and stared at Stade. I knew perfectly well that the best we could expect was that in due course our prehistoric statue would turn blue and commence to smell, but for some reason I couldn't fight off my mounting excitement. Stade's tension had got into my blood. The big doctor was trying to be the cool and collected man-of-science and failing miserably in the attempt. His eyes blazed and his big body was taught with tension. His fingers trembled as he lit a cigarette, and the half-smile on his lips was a nervous grimace, frozen there.

I chuckled. "What if he does come to life, Doc?" I asked. "You thought of that? You thought what it's going to mean to old Jimber to be fifty thousand years away from all his friends? You thought of what he may do to us?"

It was amusing to imagine that and I laughed at the notion. "What sort of people were the men of the old Stone Age?" I went on. "We named this baby after a grizzly bear and he certainly looks the part. He looks like a guy who would have definite ideas about strangers who waken people to whom they haven't been introduced—people who've been peacefully sleeping for fifty thousand years. Suppose he acts up, Doc?"

Stade shrugged. Devil-fire danced in his eyes. "Do you really think he'll come to life, Pat?" he whispered.

"You ought to know—you're the doctor."

He nodded. "Well, theoretically he should. It's not impossible . . . Come on, sit over here, Pat."

Stade bent over me, half-smiling, and his eyes burned down into mine. He didn't say anything and neither did I. Then he practically carried me across the room and propped me in a chair.

The rest of it is rather hazy. I saw it all clearly enough—I remember the whole scene now as vividly as on that day—but it was all like a vision through a pale grey veil. Like something seen through a spirit disembodied. Perhaps it was my fever and the whisky; I still don't know.

First Stade gave Big Jim a blood transfusion, using me as the donor. After that he injected an adrenalin chloride solution into the belly. The doctor crouched over the slumped body and turned a tense face to stare at me. His eyes were lambent fire. Suddenly he jerked back to his patient and I heard his startled gasp.

Jimber-Jaw opened his mouth and yawned!

I felt as if all the giants in the world had slapped me across the face. My breath caught and I couldn't see for a moment. Stade peered at me as if for confirmation, and I nodded. I have never in my life felt such a weight of responsibility. Why in the devil's name hadn't the man stayed frozen—why hadn't he started to decay? Now that he had shown signs of life we *had* to go on. It would have been murder not to finish what we started. I remember thinking dizzily: It wouldn't be right to murder a man who was born fifty thousand years ago . . .

Stade injected an ounce and a half of anterior pituitary fluid. Big Jim scowled and wiggled his fingers. He was definitely alive, and it frightened me. I almost whimpered. It was like messing around with business that belongs only to God.

Stade filled his hypodermic with posterior pituitary fluid and gave our discovery a shot of that. For a second nothing happened. Then the man of the old Stone Age turned over and tried to sit up. Stade let a yell out of him and I began to grow fainter and fainter.

As in a dream I saw Stade push him back gently and speak soothingly. I couldn't hear what he said. Then the doctor injected sex hormones from sheep and squared his shoulders triumphantly. He came towards me, eyes glowing, and about that time I passed completely out of the picture . . .

It was dark when I came to again. I had a splitting headache, my arm was sore as a boil, but otherwise I was okay again. Those fever attacks of mine have a way of vanishing swiftly. Stade was sitting at the table, shirt-sleeved, with a bottle at his elbow.

"How long have I been out?" I demanded.

"Three-four hours."

"What day is this?"

He frowned at me. "What's the matter, Pat? Have you gone completely haywire?"

I sat up—and then I saw the figure on the bench. It hadn't been a bad dream, after all. Apparently Stade had stripped the soggy skins from Jimber-Jaw, and he was wrapped in our blankets from the ship, peacefully sleeping. I went across to him and touched the bare shoulder lightly—real flesh. I could see his chest rise and fall, could hear his breathing. Slowly I went back to my home-made chair and sank down in it. I put my face in my hands and tried to think. At last I looked up and met Stade's level stare. He shrugged and nodded.

We had worked a miracle—and now we were stuck with it.

Big Jim was a fine specimen of a man, about six-feet-three and beautifully muscled. Beneath his beard he appeared to have good and regular features, though perhaps the jaw was a little heavy. Stade thought he might be in his twenties. He certainly was not old.

Some two hours later our guest from the past sat up and looked at us. A scowl darkened his forehead, and he looked about him quickly as though for his weapons. But they weren't there—Stade had seen to that. He tried to get up, but he was too weak.

"Take it easy, pal," I told him and he finally sprawled back for a while he watched us from eyes that were wide and calm and animal-alert. Then he went to sleep again.

He was a pretty sick boy for a long time. We both thought he'd never pull through. All the time we nursed him like a baby and took care of him; and by the time he commenced to convalesce he seemed to have gained confidence in us. He no longer scowled or shrank away or looked for his weapons when we came around; he smiled at us now, and it was a mighty winning smile.

At first he had been delirious; he talked a lot in a strange tongue that we couldn't make head nor tail of. A soft, liquid tongue with l's and vowels flowing through it; but low, like a deep river. There was one word that he repeated often in his delirium—*lilami*. The way he said it sounded sometimes like a prayer and sometimes like a wail of anguish.

I had repaired the carburettor. There was nothing serious the matter with it—just clogged and jammed up a little. We could have gone on as soon as our flood receded but there was Jimber-Jaw—whose name we had shortened to "Jim". We couldn't leave him to die, and he was too sick to take along; so we stayed with him. We never even discussed the matter much—just took it for granted that the responsibility was ours, and stuck along.

Stade was, of course, elated by the success of this first practical demonstration of the soundness of his theory. I don't believe you could have dragged him away from Jim with an ox team. Yet as the days went on the good doctor seemed to draw farther back into a shell of reserve. The training of our charge was mainly left to my hands.

The fact that we couldn't talk with Jim irked me. There were so many questions I wanted to ask him. Just think of it! Here was a man of the old Stone Age who could have told us all about conditions in the Pleistocene, fifty thousand years ago, perhaps; and I couldn't exchange a single thought with him. But we set out to cure that.

As soon as he was strong enough, we commenced to teach him English. At first it was aggravatingly slow work; but Jim proved an apt pupil, and as soon as he had a little foundation, he progressed rapidly. He had a marvellous memory. He never forgot anything—if he had a thing, he had it.

No use reviewing the long weeks of his convalescence and education. He recovered fully, and he learned to speak English—excellent English, for Stade was a highly cultured man and a scholar. It was just as well that Jim didn't learn his English from me—barracks and hangars are not the places to acquire academic English.

If Jim was a curiosity to us, imagine what we must have been to him. The little one-room shack we had built and in which he had convalesced was an architectural marvel beyond the limits of his imagining. He told us that his people lived in caves; and he thought that this was a strange cave that we had found, until we explained that we had built it.

Our clothing intrigued him; our weapons were a never ending source of wonderment. The first time I took him hunting with me and shot game, he was astounded. Perhaps he was frightened by the noise and the smoke and the sudden death of the quarry; but if he were, he never let on. Jim never showed fear; perhaps he never felt fear. Alone, armed only with a stone-shod spear and a stone knife, he had been hunting the great red bear when the glacier had claimed him. He told us about it.

"The day before you found me," he said, "I was hunting the great red bear. The wind blew; the snow and sleet drove against me. I could not see. I did not know in which direction I was going. I became very tired. I knew that if I lay down I should sleep and never awaken; but at last I could stand it no longer, and I lay down. If you had not come the next day, I should have died." How could we make him understand that his yesterday was fifty thousand years ago?

Eventually we succeeded in a way, though I doubt if he ever fully appreciated the tremendous lapse of time that had intervened since he started from his father's cave to hunt the great red bear.

When he first realised that he was a long way from that day and that it and his times could never be recalled, he again voiced that single word—*lilami*. It was almost a sob. I had never dreamed that so much heartache, so much longing could be encompassed within a single word.

I asked him what it meant.

He was a long time in answering. He seemed to be trying to control his emotions, which was unusual for Big Jim. Ordinarily he appeared never to have emotions. One day he told me why. A great warrior never let his face betray anger or pain or sorrow. You will notice that he didn't mention fear. Sometimes I think he had never learned what fear is. Before a youth was admitted to the warrior class, he was tortured to make certain that he could control his emotions.

But to get back to *lilami*:

At last he spoke: "Lilami is a girl—was a girl. She was to have been my mate when I came back with the head of the great red bear. Where is she now, Pat Morgan?"

There was a question! If we hadn't discovered Jim and thawed him out, Lilami wouldn't have been even a memory. "Try not to think about her, old man," I said. "You'll never see Lilami again—not in this world."

"Yes, I will," he replied. "If I am not dead, Lilami is not dead. I shall find her."

IV

_____

The plane was so absolutely beyond Jimber-Jaw's conception that he couldn't even ask questions about it. I think any one else in the world under similar circumstances, would have been terrified when we finally took off from that lonely Siberian forest. The whir of the propeller, the roar of the exhaust, the wild careening of the takeoff must have had *some* effect on Jim, but he never showed it by so much as a bat of an eyelid. He had all the appearance of a blasé young man of today.

I had given him an old suit—breeches, field boots, and a leather coat. He was smooth shaven now. After watching us scrape our jowls every day, he had insisted first on being shaved and then learning to shave himself. The transformation had been most astounding—from Man-Mountain Dean to Adonis with a few snips of the scissors and a few passes of the safety-razor!

When I looked at him and thought of the civilisation that he was about to crash for the first time, I felt sorry for Lilami. Pretty soon she would be scarcely even a memory. But I didn't know Big Jim—then.

Well, we finally got to Moscow: and there was the devil to pay about our unexpected passenger. No one believed our story. I can scarcely blame them. But what got me sore was their insistence that we were all spies and counter-revolutionists and Nazis and Fascists and capitalists and what-have-you that is anathema in Red Russia.

Of course, Jim had no passport. We tried to explain that they weren't issuing passports in the Pleistocene, but we got nowhere. They wanted to shoot us; but the American ambassador came to our rescue, and they compromised by shooing us out of the country and telling us to stay out. That suited me. If I never see a Comrade again, that will be far too soon for Pat Morgan.

After our experience in Russia, Stade and I decided to keep our mouths shut about Jim's genesis and antecedents. This was Stade's suggestion, and I confess I was rather surprised to hear him make it. The good doctor had never been averse to publicity, and here was the greatest chance in the world for him to beat his own drum. Think of the scientific *kudos* that would shower down on him!

But Stade wasn't interested in that, he said. He suddenly went coy on me—began to talk of the difficulties of establishing absolute scientific proof and all that rot. Suggested we'd better wait a while—allow our colossus to orient himself. He'd leave Jim in my care for a time, since important business was waiting for him in Chicago.

I shrugged and agreed.

We arrived in America shrouded in a pall of silence. As a matter of fact, we smuggled Jim into the USA, and after that we had to keep our mouths shut about him. What else could we have done? After all, there is no Pleistocene quota.

When we got home, I took him to my place in Beverly Hills; and told people he was an old friend—Jim Stone from Schenectady.

He had been greatly impressed by the large cities he had seen. He thought skyscrapers were mountains with caves in them. As intelligent as he was, he just couldn't conceive that man had built any thing so colossal.

It was a treat taking him around. The movies were as real to him as death and taxes. There was a caveman sequence in one we saw, and Jim really showed signs of life then. I knew he was having difficulty in restraining himself. He was just honing to crawl into one of those prop caves. When the heavy grabbed the leading lady by the hair and started to drag her across the scenery, Big Jim hoisted himself into the aisle and started for the screen. I grabbed him by the coat-tails, but it was a lap dissolve that saved the day.

Yep, Jim and I had fun . . .

One night I took him to the wrestling matches at the Olympic. We had ring-side seats. The Lone Wolf and Tiny Sawbuck (237 pounds) were committing mayhem on one another inside the ropes. It seemed to get Jim's goat.

"Do you call those great warriors?" he inquired. Then, before I could do anything about it, he vaulted over the ropes and threw them both into the third row.

The Lone Wolf and Tiny Sawbuck were sore, but the audience and the promoter were one hundred per cent plus for Jimber-Jaw. Before the evening was over, the latter had signed Jim up to meet the winner, and a week later our survivor of the Stone Age stepped into the ring with Tiny Sawbuck.

I'm still laughing. Tiny is famed as a bad hombre. He knows all the dirty tricks that the other wrestlers know and has invented quite a few of his own. But he didn't have an opportunity to try any of them on Jim. The moment they met in the centre of the ring, the man who lived in the day of the mammoths, picked him up, carried him to the ropes, and threw him into the fourth row. He did that three times, and the last time Tiny stayed there. You couldn't have hired him to come back into that ring.

About the same thing happened in boxing. I had been giving Jim some preliminary instruction in the manly art of acquiring cauliflower ears. By this time he was well known as a wrestler. Every Wednesday he had gone to the Olympic and ruined a few cash customers by throwing opponents at them. That was all he ever did. He never wrestled, never made any faces, never gave the other fellow a chance. He just picked him up and threw him out of the ring, and kept on doing it until the other man decided to stay out.

The fight promoter approached me. "Can he box?" he asked.

"I don't know. He can't wrestle, but he always wins. Why don't you find out? I have one thousand bucks that says he can put any of your white hopes to sleep."

"You're on," opined the promoter.

The following Tuesday the fight came off. I cautioned Jim: "Don't forget," I admonished him, "that you're supposed to box, not wrestle."

"I hit?" Jim inquired.

"Yes you hit—and sock him hard."

"Okey-doke," rejoined the man from the old Stone Age. "Bring 'em on!"

They shook hands and retired to their corners; then the bell rang. The white hope came charging out like the Light Brigade at Balaklava, and he got just about as far. Big Jim swung one terrific right that he must have learned from the cave-bear and the white hope was draped over the upper rope. That was the end of that fight. Others went similar ways; then the cinema moguls noticed Jimber-Jaw.

One night, while we were still negotiating for a movie contract, we went to see a preview. Lorna Downs was the star. The moment she came on to the screen, Jim sprang to his feet.

"Lilami!" he cried. "It is I, Kolani."

The heavy was insulting Lorna at the time. Jim leaped towards the screen just as Lorna made her exit into the garden. Without a moment's hesitation he tried to follow her.

It wasn't so much the damage he did to the screen as the hurt to the theatre manager's pride. He made the mistake of trying to eject Jim by force. That *was* a mistake. After they had gathered the manager up from the sidewalk and carried him to his office, I managed to settle with him and keep Jim out of jail.

When we got home, I asked Jim what it was all about.

"It was Lilami," he explained.

"It was not Lilami—it was Lorna Downs. And what you saw was not Lorna herself—just a moving picture of her."

"It was Lilami," the big fellow said gravely. "I told you that I would find her."

V

Lorna Downs was in the east making a personal appearance tour in connection with her latest release. Jim wanted to go after her. I explained that he had entered into a contract to make pictures and that he would have to live up to his agreement. I also told him that Lorna would be back in Hollywood in a few weeks, so he reluctantly agreed to wait. Meanwhile we moved into movie circles, and thus came a new phase in Jim's career. He suddenly became a social lion. Men liked him and women were crazy about him.

The first time he went to the Trocadero he turned to me and asked, "What kind of women are these?"

I told him that, measured by fame and wealth, they were the cream of the elect.

"They are without shame," he said. "They go almost naked before men. In my country their men would drag them home by the hair and beat them."

I had to admit that that was what some of our men would like to do.

"Of what good is a mate in your country?" he asked. "They are no different from men. The men smoke; the women smoke. The men drink; the women drink. The men swear; the women swear. They gamble—they tell dirty stories—they are out all night and cannot be fit to look after the caves and the children next day. They are only good for one thing, otherwise they might as well be men. One does not need to take a mate for what they can give—not here. In my country such women are killed. No one would want children from them."

The ethics, the standards, and the philosophy of the Stone Age did not fit Jim to enjoy modern society. He stopped going out evenings except to pictures and fights. He was waiting for Lilami to return.

"She is different," he said.

I felt sorry for him. I didn't know Lorna Downs, but I would have been willing to bet she was not so different.

At last Lorna came back. I was with Jim when they met. It was on a set at the studio. It was in the middle of a scene, but when he saw her he walked right off the set and up to her. Never before have I seen so much happiness and love reflected in a man's face.

"Lilami!" he said in a voice tense with emotion, and reached for her.

She shrank back. "What's the idea, big boy?" she demanded.

"Don't you know me, Lilami? I'm Kolani. Now I have found you we can go away together. I have searched for you for a long time."

She looked up at me. "Are you his keeper, mister?" she demanded. "If you are, you'd better take him back to college and lock him up."

I sent Jim away, and then I talked to her. I didn't tell her everything, but enough so that she understood that Jim wasn't crazy, that he was a good kid, and that he really believed she was the girl he had known in another country.

He was standing a little way off, and she sat and looked at him for a few moments before she answered; then she said she'd be nice to him.

"It ought to be good fun," she said.

After that they were together a great deal. It looked very much as though the movie belle were falling for the cave man. They went to shows together and dined in quiet places and took long drives.

Then, one afternoon she went to a cocktail party without him. She didn't tell him she was going; but he found it out, and along about seven o'clock he walked into the place.

Lorna was sitting on some bird's lap, and he had his arms

around her and was kissing her. It didn't mean a thing—not to them. A girl might kiss any one at a cocktail party—that is any one except her husband. But it meant a lot to Jimber-Jaw of 50,000 BC.

He was across that room in two strides. He never said a word; he just grabbed Lorna by the hair and yanked her out of the man's lap; then he picked the fellow up and threw him all the way across the room. He was the original cave man then, and no mistake.

Lorna struck down his hands and slapped his face. "Get out of here, you big boob," she screamed. "You tank-town Romeo—get out and stay out. You're washed up. I'm through with you."

Jim's fingers balled into a fist but he didn't hit her. The repressed fury drained out of his face and his shoulders sagged. He turned without a word, stalked away. That was the last time anyone ever saw him—until this morning.

Pat Morgan raised his hand, signalled to the waiter for another pair of highballs. He stared across the table at me without expression, shrugging.

"That's the story of Jimber-Jaw," he said. "Take it or leave it . . . I could see by your face when I was telling it that you were thinking what I used to think: That Stade took advantage of my grogginess—maybe even hypnotised me—to make me believe that I saw something in that Siberian hut which never happened.

"That's possible. He might have picked up some wandering dumb Kulak, put the evil eye on him, drugged him up—yes, it could have happened that way. But I don't believe it."

He tapped the newspaper that told in screaming headlines of the discovery of the body of Jim Stone. The story told of Stone's quick rise to fame, of his disappearance, of the finding of him that morning, an apparent suicide.

"But the whole story isn't there," Pat Morgan said. "The police called me in to identify the corpse, and it was Big Jim all right. They found him in the frozen-meat room of a cold storage warehouse—been there for weeks, apparently. He was resting on his side, face against his arm, and I've never seen a man, alive or dead, more peaceful.

"Pinned to the lapel of his coat was a scrawled note addressed to me. The police couldn't make head nor tail of it, but as far as I was concerned it spoke volumes. It said:

" 'I go to find the real Lilami.
And don't thaw me out again.' "

www.ingramcontent.com/pod-product-compliance
Lightning Source LLC
Chambersburg PA
CBHW030436270626
47155CB00023B/3505